THE FISHERMAN AND HIS WIFE

From the Brothers Grimm

Adapted by Heather Lee Shaw

Illustrations by Tajín Robles

Once Upon a Time in Michigan

an imprint of
MISSION POINT PRESS

Readers are encouraged to go to www.MissionPointPress.com to contact the author or to find information on how to buy this book in bulk at a discounted rate.

Adaptation and book design by Heather Lee Shaw
Illustrations by Tajín Robles

Published by Mission Point Press
2554 Chandler Rd.
Traverse City, MI 49686
(231) 421-9513
www.MissionPointPress.com

MISSION POINT PRESS

ISBN: 978-1-950659-01-2
Library of Congress Control Number: 2018967520

Printed in the United States of America.

THE FISHERMAN
AND HIS WIFE

From the Brothers Grimm

Adapted by Heather Lee Shaw
Illustrated by Tajín Robles

Once Upon a Time in Michigan

*O*nce upon a time in Michigan, a fisherman pushed his boat out upon the lake. He cast his line far across the calm water, again and again and again. "If I don't catch a fat trout or a sleek whitefish or a pretty perch, there won't be any supper tonight and my wife, Gundra, will be mad."

Suddenly, the fisherman felt a tug. He tightened his hands around the rod as something began to pull ... and pull ... AND PULL.

Out popped an enormous striped fish — a grayling fish as big as his boat. He had a red top fin and tail and his big black eye stared at the fisherman.

"**L**et me go," the fish said with a voice as deep as thunder.

The fisherman was so surprised to meet such a big fish, to hear a fish speak, that he nearly fell out of his boat.

"Let me go," the fish repeated and the sky darkened. "I am older than your grandparents and great grandparents and their parents all added together."

The fisherman thought for a moment. "Are you telling me that you're too old to eat?"

"Think what you wish," the fish said, "and grant me this favor." The sky flashed with far-away lightning.

"A favor it is, then," said the fisherman, and he carefully slid the hook out of the fish's lip. As the grayling sank back into the blue water of the lake, a trail of blood followed behind.

The fisherman pulled his boat into the trees and walked slowly down the beach. There was no point in rushing for he had no fish for supper and Gundra would be mad.

Sure enough, there she was, sitting in front of their shanty, and the minute she spotted him she began to yell. "WHAT? NO FISH? NO FOOD? YOU STUPID MAN. YOU STUPID, STUPID MAN."

"I have a story," the fisherman said, and he told her all about the giant striped grayling with its big red fin and tail.

"Tell me again what the fish said to you," Gundra demanded, poking her finger into the fisherman's neck.

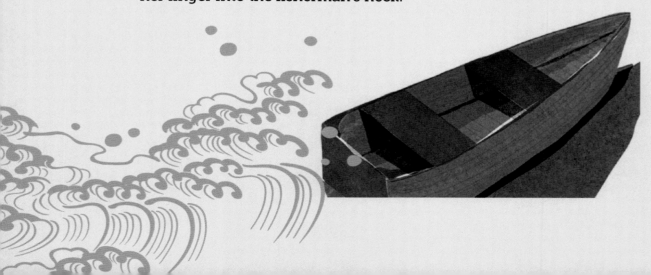

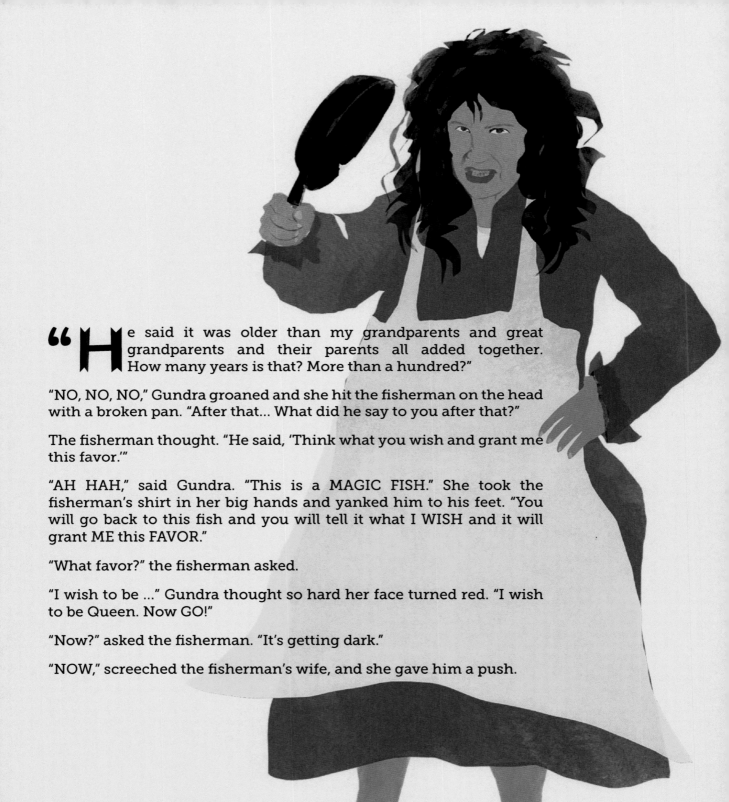

"**H**e said it was older than my grandparents and great grandparents and their parents all added together. How many years is that? More than a hundred?"

"NO, NO, NO," Gundra groaned and she hit the fisherman on the head with a broken pan. "After that... What did he say to you after that?"

The fisherman thought. "He said, 'Think what you wish and grant me this favor.'"

"AH HAH," said Gundra. "This is a MAGIC FISH." She took the fisherman's shirt in her big hands and yanked him to his feet. "You will go back to this fish and you will tell it what I WISH and it will grant ME this FAVOR."

"What favor?" the fisherman asked.

"I wish to be ..." Gundra thought so hard her face turned red. "I wish to be Queen. Now GO!"

"Now?" asked the fisherman. "It's getting dark."

"NOW," screeched the fisherman's wife, and she gave him a push.

The fisherman walked slowly back down the beach. He pulled his boat out of the trees and pushed it once again out upon the water, water so flat and still that the stars and moon shone above and below. He rowed and rowed. When the darkness was all around him, the fisherman rested his oars and called to the fish:

"Grayling, grayling, hear her wish,
Gundra asks a favor of the fish."

The wind came up and the fisherman felt his hair lift off his forehead. Clouds covered the moon and stars. Little waves kicked his boat back and forth. The grayling's enormous head rose above the surface of the lake. His big red fin unfolded. His big black eye flashed.

"What does Gundra want?" the fish roared in his voice of thunder.

"She wants to be Queen," the fisherman said.

"Go home, man. It is done."

The sun was just peeking over the hill when the fisherman approached his home. His mouth dropped open. His eyes popped. Gone was the old shanty, and in its place stood a palace made of blossoms. Red cherries, black cherries, yellow cherries swirled in carpets and curtains. Right in the middle of the palace was a chair made of green and red branches, and on the chair sat the fisherman's wife in a blossom-white dress and a golden crown of bees. Nothing surprised the fisherman more, though, than when Gundra spoke. In a soft voice she said, "Why, look at this. Isn't this nice?"

The fisherman smiled and nodded. "I hope you can be happy now, my wife."

Gundra sniffed. "We shall see."

And for three whole months they were happy: April, May and June. But when the spring cherries ripened and fell to the ground, Gundra began to growl. She grabbed the fisherman by his ears and yanked him to his feet. "I am bored of being Queen. You will go back to this fish and you will tell it what I WISH and it will grant ME this FAVOR."

"Another favor?" the fisherman asked. "What favor?"

"I wish to be..." Gundra thought so hard her face turned red. "I wish to be Empress. Now GO!"

"Now?" asked the fisherman. "It's getting dark."

"NOW," screeched the fisherman's wife, and she gave him a push.

The fisherman walked slowly down the beach. He pulled his boat out of the trees and pushed it out upon the water, water so flat and still that the stars and moon shone above and below. He rowed and rowed, and when the darkness was all around him, he rested his oars and called to the fish:

> "Grayling, grayling, hear her wish,
> Gundra asks a favor of the fish."

The wind came up and the fisherman's hat flew off his head. Clouds raced over the moon and stars. Whitecaps slapped his boat back and forth. The grayling's enormous head rose above the surface of the lake. His big red fin unfolded. His big black eye flashed.

"What does Gundra want?" the fish roared in its voice of thunder.

"I am sorry. She is bored of being a queen. She wants to be Empress," the fisherman said.

"Go home, man. It is done."

The sun was just peeking over the hill when the fisherman approached his home. His mouth dropped open. His eyes popped. Gone was the palace of blossoms and in its place stood a castle as high as the sky. Its walls were the color of sand. There were towers of sand and battlements of sand. There were caves and peaks and pools of golden sand. The fisherman climbed the sand stairs to the top of the sand castle, and there, in the very middle, was a throne of grape vines and on the throne sat the fisherman's wife in a purple robe and a crown of shining grape leaves. Nothing surprised the fisherman more, though, than when Gundra spoke. In a soft voice she said, "Why, look at this. Isn't this nice?"

The fisherman nodded and smiled. "I hope you can be happy now, my wife."

"We shall see," Gundra sniffed

And for three whole months they were happy: July, August and September. But when the summer grapes ripened and fell to the ground, Gundra began to growl. She gathered the fisherman's hair in her big hands and yanked him to his feet. "I am bored of being Empress. You will go back to this fish and you will tell it what I WISH and it will grant ME this FAVOR."

"Another favor my wife?" the fisherman asked. "What favor this time?"

"I wish to be..." Gundra thought so hard her face turned purple. "I wish to be President. Now GO!"

"Now?" asked the fisherman. "It's getting dark."

"NOW," screeched the fisherman's wife, and she gave him a push.

Empress of Leelanau

The fisherman walked slowly down the beach. He pulled his boat out of the trees and pushed it out upon the water, water so flat and still that the stars and moon shone above and below. He rowed and rowed. When the darkness was all around him, the fisherman rested his oars and called to the fish:

"Grayling, grayling, hear her wish,
Gundra asks a favor of the fish."

The wind came up and the fisherman's eyes stung with hard rain. Clouds boiled over the moon and stars. Thick black waves threw his canoe back and forth. The grayling's enormous head rose above the boat. His big red fin unfolded. His big black eye flashed.

"Now what does Gundra want?" the fish roared in its voice of thunder.

"I am so sorry to bother you, but Gundra is bored of being an empress. She wants to be President," the fisherman said.

"Go home, man. It is done."

Leelanau

The sun was just peeking over the hill when the fisherman approached his home. His mouth dropped open. His eyes popped. Gone was the sand castle and in its place a bridge arched up like a rainbow. The fisherman climbed the rainbow to the top of the hill. On and on the rainbow stretched, from peninsula to peninsula. In the very middle, like the sun in a rain shower, perched a golden house. There were columns and domes of yellow and orange. There were gardens of scarlet flowers. Black swans swam in pools of silver. Standing in the doorway, with eagles on either side, stood the fisherman's wife. She wore a black suit with golden buttons. Medals on chains of gold hung from her neck. Nothing surprised the fisherman more, though, than when Gundra spoke. In a soft voice she said, "Why, look at this. Isn't this nice?"

The fisherman nodded. "I hope you can be happy now, my wife."

Gundra sniffed. "We shall see."

And for three whole months they were happy: October, November and December. But when the fall leaves ripened and fell to the ground, Gundra began to growl. With her huge hands she pinched the fisherman by his shoulders and yanked him to his feet. "I am bored with being President," she said. "You will go back to this fish and you will tell it what I WISH and it will grant ME this FAVOR."

"Yet another favor," the fisherman said. "What favor this time?"

"I wish to be…" Gundra thought so hard her face turned black. "I wish to be Lord. Now GO!"

"Now?" asked the fisherman. "It's getting dark."

"NOW," screeched the fisherman's wife, and she gave him a push.

President of the Peninsulas

Old Mission

The fisherman walked slowly, sadly down the beach. He pulled his boat out of the trees and pushed it out upon the water, water so flat and still that the stars and moon shone above and below. He rowed and rowed. When the darkness was all around him, the fisherman rested his oars and called to the fish:

"Grayling, grayling, hear her wish,
Gundra asks a favor of the fish."

Clouds fell down across the moon and stars. The wind roared like a train. Frozen rain whipped at his cheeks and stuck to his hair and eyelashes.

Greasy gray waves rocked his boat sickeningly.
The grayling's enormous head rose above the surface of
the lake. His big red fin unfolded. His big black eye flashed

"What does Gundra want now?" the fish roared in its voice of
thunder.

"I am so, so sorry," the fisherman shouted above the storm.
"Gundra is bored with being a president. She wants to be Lord."

"Go home, man. It is done."

Lord of the Lakes

The sun was just peeking over the hill when the fisherman approached his home. But no one was there. Nothing was there but ice and snow. The fisherman shaded his eyes and looked to the top of the hill: nothing. He looked up the beach and down the beach: nothing. He looked out across the frozen lake. His mouth dropped open. His eyes popped. There, on the ice, he saw a mountain. The mountain was his wife, Gundra.

The fisherman walked and walked. The closer he got to her, the bigger she was. Gundra's head was as big as an air balloon and each of her toes was bigger than a boat.

When Gundra said, "Why, look at this. Isn't this nice?" the fisherman was not surprised, but he nodded and tried to smile. "I hope you can be happy now, my wife."

The mountain of Gundra sniffed. "We shall see."

And for three whole months Gundra sat on the ice, the Lord of the Lakes: January, February and March. But when the ice began to groan and the sun began to warm and the wind began to bring the little birds, Gundra began to growl. She scooped up her fisherman husband in her hand as big as a bus and said, "I am bored of being Lord. You will go back to this fish and you will tell it what I WISH and it will grant ME this FAVOR."

"Not another favor," the fisherman said. "I am afraid to ask for another favor."

"BE AFRAID OF ME," Gundra howled. "I've been Queen and Empress and President and Lord, but that is not enough. The wind still blows as it wishes, the sun still shines where it will, the rain and snow come whether I ask them to or not... I wish to be..." Gundra thought and thought. She thought so hard her face turned white. "I wish to be like the sun, the wind, the snow, the rain. I wish to be everything and everywhere. Now GO!"

The fisherman walked slowly, slowly back across the ice. He walked slowly, slowly down the beach. He pulled his boat out of the trees and pushed it toward the water. To his surprise, blue birds flew around his head and a bright fish swam around his boat. The fisherman was puzzled by the bright weather, but he rowed and rowed. At last, he rested his oars and called to the fish:

"Grayling, grayling, hear her wish,
Gundra asks a favor of the fish."

The grayling's enormous head rose above the surface of the lake. His big red fin unfolded. His big black eye flashed.

"What does Gundra want?" the fish roared in his voice of thunder.

The fisherman took a deep breath. "She wants to be like the sun and the wind, the rain and the snow," he said. "She wants to be everything and everywhere."

A crack like thunder split the sky. A soaking rain made a gray curtain all around the fisherman and the fish. Then the sun exploded through the clouds – the rain stopped, the bright fish and little birds returned.

"Go home, man," said the graying. "It is done."

And the fisherman went home. He ran down the beach, and the sun, just peeking over the hill, shone warmly on his head. The wind blew gently, smelling of cherry blossoms. There was his old shanty. There was his chair and the broken pan. But where was Gundra?

The fisherman shaded his eyes and looked far out across the lake. The water licked at the sandy beach. The ice was gone, the mountain was gone. The fisherman nodded and smiled and said to himself, "Why, look at this. Isn't this nice?"

Gundra was the sun and wind. She was the rain and the snow. She was everywhere and everything, and it was good.

The End.

Philipp Otto Runge,
self portrait, ca 1802

ABOUT THE STORY

"The Fisherman and His Wife" was originally published
by Philipp Otto Runge in 1808. Runge had been a sickly
child, and he may have first heard the story during the
long periods he spent at home, away from school.

Runge grew up in West Pomeriania, a land now split
between Germany and Poland. Pomeriania is known
for its sandy beaches along the Baltic Sea and, in fact,
its comes from the Slavic, meaning "land by the sea."
Runge's life was short, but he is considered one of the
most accomplished of the German Romantic painters.

In 1812, "The Fisherman and His Wife" was collected
by the Brothers Grimm. Since then the fable has been
adapted many times: Aleksandr Pushkin used the
theme in a poem in 1833; Nobel Prize-winner Gunter
Grass based his novel, The Flounder, on the fable; as
did Ursula LeGuin in her novel The Lathe of Heaven.

Once Upon a Time in Michigan is a series of children's books published by Mission Point Press. The stories are old family favorites, based in Michigan. The first in the series, The Fisherman and His Wife is located in the Grand Traverse region. The second book, City Raccoon, Country Raccoon, takes place in Detroit and Tahquamenon Falls.

ABOUT THE AUTHOR
Heather Lee Shaw grew up on a cherry farm in Yuba, Michigan. She is a partner in Mission Point Press and the author of Inside UpNorth: The Complete Tour, Sport and Country Living Guide to Traverse City, Traverse City Area and Leelanau County.

ABOUT THE ILLUSTRATOR
Tajín Robles was born in San Cristóbal de Las Casas, Chiapas, Mexico. When still a child, his family moved to Traverse City, although he continued to spend summers in Mexico. This is Tajín's second illustrated book; the first is Aiden's Tree: The Story of a Fir Tree, a Boy and the Mackinac Ice Bridge. Find his work at TajinRobles.com.